Dear Parent:

Remember the first time you read a book by yourself? I do.
I still remember the thrill of reading the words Little Bear said
to Mother Bear: "I have a new space helmet. I am going to
the moon."

Later when my daughter was
learning to read, her favorite I
Can Read books were the funny
ones—Danny playing with the
dinosaur he met at the museum
and Amelia Bedelia dressing
the chicken. And now as a new
teacher, she has joined the
thousands of teachers who use
I Can Read books in the classroom.

I'm delighted to share this commemorative edition with you.
This special volume includes the origin stories and early sketches
of many beloved I Can Read characters.

Here's to the next sixty years—and to all those beginning
readers who are about to embark on a lifetime of discovery that
starts with the magical words *"I can read!"*

Kate M. Jackson
Senior VP, Associate Publisher, Editor-in-Chief

Frog and Toad Are Friends

by Arnold Lobel

An I CAN READ Book®

HARPER

An Imprint of HarperCollins*Publishers*

For Barbara Borack

I Can Read Book® is a trademark of HarperCollins Publishers.

Frog and Toad Are Friends Copyright © 1970 by Arnold Lobel.

Library of Congress Cataloging Card Number: 73-105492
ISBN 978-0-06-257273-8

17 18 19 20 PC/WOR 10 9 8 7 6 5   ❖   Originally published in 1970

Contents

Spring

Frog ran up the path
to Toad's house.
He knocked on the front door.
There was no answer.
"Toad, Toad," shouted Frog,
"wake up. It is spring!"
"Blah," said a voice
from inside the house.
"Toad, Toad," cried Frog.

"The sun is shining!

The snow is melting. Wake up!"

"I am not here," said the voice.

Frog walked into the house.

It was dark.

All the shutters were closed.

"Toad, where are you?" called Frog.

"Go away," said the voice
from a corner of the room.

Toad was lying in bed.

He had pulled all the covers

over his head.

Frog pushed Toad out of bed.

He pushed him out of the house

and onto the front porch.

Toad blinked in the bright sun.

"Help!" said Toad.

"I cannot see anything."

"Don't be silly," said Frog.

"What you see

is the clear warm light of April.

And it means

that we can begin

a whole new year together, Toad.

Think of it," said Frog.

"We will skip through the meadows

and run through the woods

and swim in the river.

In the evenings we will sit

right here on this front porch

and count the stars."

"You can count them, Frog,"
said Toad. "I will be too tired.
I am going back to bed."

Toad went back into the house.

He got into the bed

and pulled the covers

over his head again.

"But, Toad," cried Frog,

"you will miss all the fun!"

"Listen, Frog," said Toad.

"How long have I been asleep?"

"You have been asleep
since November," said Frog.
"Well then," said Toad,
"a little more sleep
will not hurt me.
Come back again and wake me up
at about half past May.
Good night, Frog."

"But, Toad," said Frog,

"I will be lonely until then."

Toad did not answer.

He had fallen asleep.

Frog looked at Toad's calendar.

The November page was still on top.

Frog tore off the November page.

He tore off the December page.

And the January page,

the February page,

and the March page.

He came to the April page.

Frog tore off the April page too.

Then Frog ran back to Toad's bed.

"Toad, Toad, wake up. It is May now."

"What?" said Toad.

"Can it be May so soon?"

"Yes," said Frog.

"Look at your calendar."

Toad looked at the calendar.

The May page was on top.

"Why, it *is* May!" said Toad
as he climbed out of bed.
Then he and Frog
ran outside
to see how the world
was looking in the spring.

The Story

One day in summer
Frog was not feeling well.
Toad said, "Frog,
you are looking quite green."
"But I always look green,"
said Frog. "I am a frog."
"Today you look very green
even for a frog," said Toad.
"Get into my bed and rest."

Toad made Frog a cup of hot tea.

Frog drank the tea, and then he said,

"Tell me a story while I am resting."

"All right," said Toad.

"Let me think of a story to tell you."

Toad thought and thought.

But he could not think of a story

to tell Frog.

18

"I will go out on the front porch
and walk up and down," said Toad.
"Perhaps that will help me
to think of a story."
Toad walked up and down
on the porch for a long time.
But he could not think of a story
to tell Frog.

Then Toad went into the house

and stood on his head.

"Why are you standing

on your head?" asked Frog.

"I hope that if I stand on my head,

it will help me

to think of a story," said Toad.

Toad stood on his head

for a long time.

But he could not think

of a story to tell Frog.

Then Toad poured a glass of water
over his head.

"Why are you pouring water
over your head?" asked Frog.

"I hope that if I pour water
over my head,

it will help me to think
of a story," said Toad.

Toad poured many glasses of water
over his head.

But he could not think
of a story to tell Frog.

Then Toad began
to bang his head
against the wall.

"Why are you banging your head
against the wall?" asked Frog.
"I hope that if I bang my head
against the wall hard enough,
it will help me to think of a story,"
said Toad.

"I am feeling much better now, Toad,"
said Frog. "I do not think
I need a story anymore."
"Then you get out of bed
and let me get into it," said Toad,
"because now I feel terrible."
Frog said, "Would you like me
to tell you a story, Toad?"
"Yes," said Toad, "if you know one."

"Once upon a time," said Frog,

"there were two good friends,

a frog and a toad.

The frog was not feeling well.

He asked his friend the toad

to tell him a story.

The toad could not think of a story.

He walked up and down on the porch,

but he could not think of a story.

He stood on his head,

but he could not think of a story.

He poured water over his head,

but he could not think of a story.

He banged his head against the wall,

but he still could not think

of a story.

Then the toad did not feel so well,

and the frog was feeling better.

So the toad went to bed

and the frog got up

and told him a story.

The end.

How was that,

Toad?" said Frog.

But Toad did not answer.

He had fallen asleep.

A Lost Button

Toad and Frog
went for a long walk.
They walked across
a large meadow.
They walked in the woods.
They walked along the river.
At last they went back home
to Toad's house.
"Oh, drat," said Toad.

"Not only do my feet hurt,

but I have lost

one of the buttons on my jacket."

"Don't worry," said Frog.

"We will go back

to all the places where we walked.

We will soon find your button."

They walked back to the large meadow.

They began to look for the button

in the tall grass.

"Here is your button!" cried Frog.

"That is not my button," said Toad.

"That button is black.

My button was white."

Toad put the black button

in his pocket.

A sparrow flew down.

"Excuse me," said the sparrow.

"Did you lose a button? I found one."

"That is not my button," said Toad.

"That button has two holes.

My button had four holes."

Toad put the button with two holes

in his pocket.

They went back to the woods
and looked on the dark paths.
"Here is your button," said Frog.
"That is not my button," cried Toad.
"That button is small.
My button was big."
Toad put the small button
in his pocket.

A raccoon came out from behind a tree.

"I heard that you were looking

for a button," he said.

"Here is one that I just found."

"That is not my button!" wailed Toad.

"That button is square.

My button was round."

Toad put the square button

in his pocket.

Frog and Toad went back to the river.

They looked for the button

in the mud.

"Here is your button," said Frog.

"That is not my button!" shouted Toad.

"That button is thin.

My button was thick."

Toad put the thin button
in his pocket. He was very angry.
He jumped up and down
and screamed,
"The whole world
is covered with buttons,
and not one of them is mine!"

Toad ran home and slammed the door.

There, on the floor,

he saw his white, four-holed,

big, round, thick button.

"Oh," said Toad.

"It was here all the time.

What a lot of trouble

I have made for Frog."

Toad took all of the buttons
out of his pocket.
He took his sewing box
down from the shelf.
Toad sewed the buttons
all over his jacket.

The next day Toad gave

his jacket to Frog.

Frog thought that it was beautiful.

He put it on and jumped for joy.

None of the buttons fell off.

Toad had sewed them on very well.

A Swim

Toad and Frog
went down to the river.
"What a day for a swim," said Frog.
"Yes," said Toad.
"I will go behind these rocks
and put on my bathing suit."
"I don't wear a bathing suit,"
said Frog.
"Well, I do," said Toad.

"After I put on my bathing suit,
you must not look at me
until I get into the water."

"Why not?"

asked Frog.

"Because I look funny

in my bathing suit.

That is why," said Toad.

Frog closed his eyes when Toad

came out from behind the rocks.

Toad was wearing his bathing suit.

"Don't peek," he said.

Frog and Toad jumped
into the water.
They swam all afternoon.
Frog swam fast
and made big splashes.
Toad swam slowly
and made smaller splashes.

A turtle came along the riverbank.

"Frog, tell that turtle

to go away," said Toad.

"I do not want him to see me

in my bathing suit

when I come out of the river."

Frog swam over to the turtle.

"Turtle," said Frog,

"you will have to go away."

"Why should I?" asked the turtle.

"Because Toad thinks that

he looks funny in his bathing suit,

and he does not want you to see him,"

said Frog.

Some lizards were sitting nearby.

"Does Toad really look funny

in his bathing suit?" they asked.

A snake crawled out of the grass.

"If Toad looks funny

in his bathing suit," said the snake,

"then I, for one, want to see him."

"We want to see him too,"
said two dragonflies.

"Me too," said a field mouse.
"I have not seen anything funny
in a long time."

Frog swam back to Toad.

"I am sorry, Toad," he said. "Everyone wants to see how you will look."

"Then I will stay right here until they go away," said Toad.

The turtle and the lizards and the snake and the dragonflies and the field mouse all sat on the riverbank.

They waited for Toad to come out of the water.

"Please," cried Frog, "please go away!"

But no one went away.

Toad was getting colder and colder.

He was beginning to shiver and sneeze.

"I will have to come out of the water,"

said Toad. "I am catching a cold."

Toad climbed
out of the river.
The water dripped
out of his bathing suit
and down onto his feet.

The turtle laughed.

The lizards laughed.

The snake laughed.

The field mouse laughed,

and Frog laughed.

"What are you laughing at, Frog?"
said Toad.

"I am laughing at you, Toad,"
said Frog,

"because you *do* look funny
in your bathing suit."

"Of course I do," said Toad.
Then he picked up his clothes
and went home.

The Letter

Toad was sitting on his front porch.

Frog came along and said,

"What is the matter, Toad?

You are looking sad."

"Yes," said Toad.

"This is my sad time of day.

It is the time

when I wait for the mail to come.

It always makes me very unhappy."

"Why is that?" asked Frog.

"Because I never get any mail,"

said Toad.

"Not ever?" asked Frog.

"No, never," said Toad.

"No one has ever sent me a letter.

Every day my mailbox is empty.

That is why waiting for the mail

is a sad time for me."

Frog and Toad sat on the porch,

feeling sad together.

Then Frog said,

"I have to go home now, Toad.

There is something that I must do."

Frog hurried home.

He found a pencil

and a piece of paper.

He wrote on the paper.

He put the paper in an envelope.

On the envelope he wrote

"A LETTER FOR TOAD."

Frog ran out of his house.

He saw a snail that he knew.

"Snail," said Frog, "please take

this letter to Toad's house

and put it in his mailbox."

"Sure," said the snail. "Right away."

Then Frog ran back to Toad's house.

Toad was in bed, taking a nap.

"Toad," said Frog,

"I think you should get up

and wait for the mail some more."

"No," said Toad,

"I am tired of waiting for the mail."

Frog looked out of the window
at Toad's mailbox.
The snail was not there yet.
"Toad," said Frog, "you never know
when someone may send you a letter."
"No, no," said Toad. "I do not think
anyone will ever send me a letter."

Frog looked out of the window.

The snail was not there yet.

"But, Toad," said Frog,

"someone may send you a letter today."

"Don't be silly," said Toad.

"No one has ever sent me

a letter before, and no one

will send me a letter today."

Frog looked out of the window.

The snail was still not there.

"Frog, why do you keep looking

out of the window?" asked Toad.

"Because now I am waiting

for the mail," said Frog.

"But there will not be any," said Toad.

"Oh, yes there will," said Frog,

"because I have sent you a letter."

"You have?" said Toad.

"What did you write in the letter?"

Frog said, "I wrote

'Dear Toad, I am glad

that you are my best friend.

Your best friend, Frog.'"

"Oh," said Toad,

"that makes a very good letter."

Then Frog and Toad went out

onto the front porch

to wait for the mail.

They sat there,

feeling happy together.

Frog and Toad waited a long time.

Four days later

the snail got to Toad's house

and gave him the letter from Frog.

Toad was very pleased to have it.

"I can read! I can read!
Where are the books for me?"

One question from a young reader sparked a reading revolution!

A conversation between the director of Harper's Department of Books for Boys and Girls, Ursula Nordstrom, and Boston Public Library's Virginia Haviland inspired the I Can Read book series. Haviland told Nordstrom that a young boy had burst into the children's reading room and asked her where he could find books that were just right for a brand-new reader like himself.

Determined to fill this gap, Nordstrom published *Little Bear* by Else Holmelund Minarik, with illustrations by Maurice Sendak, in the fall of 1957. The response was immediate. According to the *New York Times*, "One look at the illustrations and children will grab for it. A second look at the short, easy sentences, the repetition of words, and the beautiful type spacing, and children will know they can read it themselves."

Delightful and wonderfully warm, *Little Bear* served as the template for the series, and now, sixty years later, we have over four hundred I Can Read stories for our youngest and newest readers!

Berenstain Bears

Stan and Jan Berenstain were cartoonists in the 1950s. When their sons began to read, they submitted a story about a family of bears to author, editor, and publisher Ted Geisel (aka Dr. Seuss), which was published as *The Big Honey Hunt* in 1962. Geisel labeled their next effort "Another Adventure of the Berenstain Bears." That's how the bears got their name!

Biscuit

One day while watching her daughter play with their neighbor's frisky dog, Alyssa Capucilli was struck by her daughter's patience and gentle nature, as well as the fact that her little girl thought the dog understood every word she said. That was the inspiration for the little yellow puppy and his sweet companion. Pat Schories's warm illustrations capture their tender relationship.

Pete the Cat

When James Dean first saw Pete, he was a tiny black kitten in a shelter. Pete looked like he had been starved and his black fur was a mess. At first, James had no interest in Pete—black cats were bad luck, after all! But the scrawny little fellow stuck his paw out of the cage, wanting to play! James took Pete home. And even though James chose to paint Pete the Cat blue (his favorite color), James realizes now that black cats are actually very good luck.

Danny and the Dinosaur

In 1958, cartoonist Syd Hoff's daughter Susan was going through a rough surgery, and one day, Syd decided to draw a picture to cheer her up. It showed a dinosaur with Syd's brother on its back. When Susie saw the picture, she exclaimed, "Danny and the dinosaur!" and that night after the family went to bed, Syd wrote the story.

Pinkalicious

Victoria Kann's daughters could never seem to get enough of cupcakes or the color pink! One year, as an April Fools' joke, Victoria told her family and friends that one of her daughters had turned pink from eating too many pink cupcakes—and so the idea for *Pinkalicious* was born!

Frog and Toad

The characters of Frog and his best friend, Toad, might have been inspired by . . . a horror movie! Arnold Lobel and his daughter, Adrianne, went to see a movie called *Frogs* at the drive-in. However, the movie featured not frogs, but toads! Adrianne told her dad about the many differences between the two—and two years later the first Frog and Toad book, *Frog and Toad Are Friends*, appeared.

Little Critter

Mercer Mayer was doodling around one day in 1974 when he drew a shape like a gourd, put two eyes on it, scribbled a nose connecting the eyes, then got coffee and forgot about it! The next day, he noticed a small piece of paper on the floor. It was his gourd. He added fuzzy hair and a big mouth; short stubby arms and feet. Mercer had created a fuzzy little "woodchuck-y porcupine" thing that became Little Critter!

Fancy Nancy

When Jane O'Connor was a small girl, every Sunday, when her grandma and great aunts came to visit, Jane would greet them at the door in a tutu and a pair of her mom's high heels. She thought she looked très glamorous!

Years later, while she was fixing dinner one night, the name Fancy Nancy flew into Jane's head, and a star made her debut!

Amelia Bedelia

Amelia Bedelia was inspired by Peggy Parish's third-grade students at the Dalton School in New York City. The children mixed up words, and Parish found them hilarious. That gave Parish the idea for Amelia Bedelia—a character who takes every word literally and embraces life with an outlook that is forthright and optimistic. Illustrator Fritz Siebel worked with Parish to create the perfect look for the conscientious cleaning lady.

Early Character Development

The Berenstain Bears

Stan and Jan Berenstain's early sketches from *The Berenstain Bears Clean House*

Pete the Cat

Frog and Toad
Early character sketch of Frog and Toad

James Dean's first painting of Pete the Cat

JAMES DEAN
12. 26. 99

Biscuit

Biscuit character sketches

Pat Schories's early sketches from *Biscuit*

Pinkalicious

Victoria Kann's sketches for the picture book *Pinkalicious*

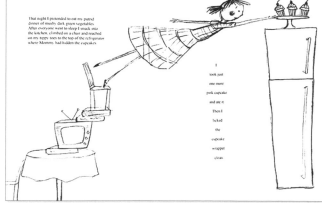

Amelia Bedelia

Fritz Siebel's sketches for the picture book *Amelia Bedelia*

Danny and the Dinosaur

Syd Hoff's early cover sketches for *Danny and the Dinosaur*

Little Critter

Mercer Mayer's early character sketches of Little Critter

Fancy Nancy

Robin Preiss Glasser's character sketches and cover sketch for *Fancy Nancy and the Boy from Paris*

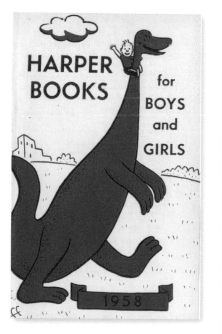

These two catalogs marked the launch of I Can Read!

Sixty Years of I CAN READ

1957
Little Bear

1958
Danny and the Dinosaur

1959
Sammy the Seal

Emmett's Pig

1960
Cat and Dog

1961
Little Bear's Visit*

1963
Amelia Bedelia

1970
Frog and Toad Are Friends*

A Bargain for Frances

1972
Frog and Toad Together**

1984
In a Dark, Dark Room and Other Scary Stories

1986
The Josefina Story Quilt

1996
Biscuit

2005
The Berenstain Bears Clean House

2008
Fancy Nancy and the Boy from Paris

Little Critter: Snowball Soup

2010
Pinkalicious: School Rules!

2013
Pete the Cat: Pete's Big Lunch

2017
Long, Tall Lincoln

* Caldecott Honor titles
** Newbery Honor